A WISH AND A PRAYER

A Novella

ROBIN LEE HATCHER

A Wish and a Prayer

A WISH AND A PRAYER

by

ROBIN LEE HATCHER

Prologue

Idaho, 1897

Having four legs and claws had its benefits, Angel Emeline decided as she scratched a hard-to-reach spot with her hind leg. But she would never admit it to Archie. If she did, the Archangel in Charge of Prayer Assistance might always give her this sort of assignment. And next time, he might send her into a less desirable creature than the noble cat.

When the itch was gone at last, Angel Emeline straightened and looked about her, wanting to get acquainted with her surroundings. The small house was simple, attractive, and tidy. She'd have expected nothing less from Miss Felicity Blessing of Appleton, Idaho.

Felicity was a dressmaker, a woman of thirty, never married. She'd lived in this house since the day she was born and had cared for her father—a drinker of strong spirits—after losing her mother eighteen years ago. The task had become particularly difficult after Samuel Blessing, drunk as usual, fell from a moving wagon, crippling his right leg and leaving him mean and bitter, a bitterness he'd taken out on his daughter until the day he died. That was the sum of what Angel Emeline had learned about Miss Felicity Blessing before arriving on earth in answer to her prayers.

The door opened, allowing golden sunlight to spill across the rag rug seconds before the subject of Angel Emeline's thoughts entered the house. Felicity's mahogany-colored hair was pulled back from her face in a severe twist and was topped with a straw hat that had nary a speck of decoration. Her tan and brown linen shirtwaist and skirt were equally plain and dull. Not even a bit of lace to lessen the severity.

My, my, Miss Blessing. However am I to help you if you don't help yourself?

For a moment, Angel Emeline wondered if this was a job too big for an Angel, Third Grade, to handle. But handle it she must if she wanted her promotion.

With a mental nod, she rose, arched her back, and meowed for attention.

Chapter 1

Felicity pulled the long hat pin from her bonnet as she glanced at the white cat standing on the sofa.

"Hello, Angel. Are you hungry?"

She dropped her straw hat onto the table near the door, then crossed the room and lifted the feline into her arms, rubbing her cheek against Angel's long, soft coat.

"Mrs. Babcock gave me two more orders today. The work will pay enough to see us through the month." A sigh escaped her. "But I don't suppose you worry about such things, do you? It must be nice not to have a worry in the world."

She stroked the cat, remembering how empty her house had seemed before Angel came calling at her back door, a tiny, miserable-looking kitten with a matted coat and a voracious appetite. Felicity hadn't been as lonely since that stormy night over a year ago.

Not *as* lonely ... but still lonely.

With another sigh, she set the cat on the floor and walked into the kitchen where she put the kettle on for tea.

Long ago, when she'd still believed wishes could come true, she'd wished for someone to talk to, someone who could talk back once in a while, someone to dispel the silence. Her throat tightened. Once, when she'd still believed in answered prayers, she'd prayed for someone to love her, someone she could love in return.

Angel brushed up against her skirts. Felicity smiled sadly as she glanced down. "You've always loved me, haven't you, pet?" Then she frowned.

Self-pity was most unbecoming, and it wasn't like her to give in to it. She'd chosen to be the mistress of her own life. She hadn't wanted to marry. After her father died, she hadn't wanted to give up her newfound freedom. She liked making her own decisions. Angel was all the family she needed.

And it wasn't as if Felicity had never had an opportunity to marry. She'd received a few proposals over the years. Women were at a premium in these parts, and even a plain-faced one like Felicity was desirable to a widower with a cold bed and half-a-dozen children who needed tending.

"Don't marry for any reason but love, Felicity." It had been eighteen years since her mother spoke those words to her, but it seemed like only yesterday. *"Better to be an old maid than to marry for less than love."*

The kettle began to whistle, intruding on her unhappy memories.

"I won't feel sorry for myself," she muttered as she reached for the delicate china cup she used when she was blue. "I won't."

"Reow."

Once again, she glanced down. Angel sat and cocked her head to one side, as if questioning her mistress. A laugh rose in Felicity's throat. So this was what she'd come to. Talking to her cat while puttering around the kitchen. There was no doubt about it.

She *was* an old maid.

PRESCOTT JONES RODE his buckskin gelding along the wide, dusty main street of Appleton. It was an ordinary Western town—two churches, a mercantile, red-brick bank, one saloon, dress shop, a doctor, small schoolhouse. Just about everything the citizens of a town might need. Even its own newspaper.

But one thing was missing, especially for a place surrounded by acre upon acre of fruit orchards. A cannery.

Prescott was there to rectify that omission.

He pulled on the reins when he saw the small shingle announcing his destination: Walter L. Johnson, Attorney-at-Law. He swung down from the saddle, wrapped the reins around the hitching post, then stepped onto the boardwalk.

Once more he glanced down the length of the town. He liked what he saw. There was potential for growth here, potential for a good life if a person was willing to work for it. It was a place where a man could put down roots, take a wife, start a family. To Prescott, nothing sounded better. He'd been alone too long. He wanted to belong—to some place and to someone.

Without further hesitation, he opened the door to the office and stepped inside.

His boyhood friend stared down at his desk, squinting through thick glasses at a sheet of white paper filled with small print. The past twenty-five years hadn't changed Walt much. He was still slight and wiry, just as he'd been as a boy at the orphanage. Even the familiar smattering of freckles over the bridge of his nose was the same. The only sign of his real age of thirty-five was the touch of gray at his temples.

"I'll be with you in a moment," Walt said, still studying the papers before him.

"No hurry. I'm here to stay."

Walt glanced up, and at the moment of recognition, his mouth curved into a welcoming smile. "Prescott! I wasn't expecting you for another week." He rose from his chair and stepped around the desk.

They clasped upper arms as they stared at one another, finding the boys they remembered behind the faces of the men they'd become. The years melted away, and memories of Prescott's childhood flickered through his head.

"It's good to see you, Pres. Been a long time."

"Too long."

"I'm glad you decided to come."

"So am I." He released his grip on Walt's arms, then removed his dusty Stetson and tossed it onto a nearby chair. Raking his fingers through his hair, he asked, "Have you bought the property?"

"Most of it."

Prescott raised an eyebrow in question.

His friend motioned to another chair. "Sit down. I'll tell you all about it." Walt moved around his desk. When they were both seated, he continued, "I've heard from the railroad. They're close to making a decision. I think they'll bring the spur this way regardless, but a cannery will clinch the deal. They won't have to worry about all that fruit spoiling if anything slows down delivery to markets."

Walt wasn't saying anything Prescott didn't already know. "And the property?"

"I found the perfect location on the far end of town, like I told you in my last letter." Walt motioned with his hand toward the west. "I've been able to buy all the lots we'll need ... except one. There's a house on it, and the woman who lives there refuses to sell." He frowned. "Problem is, it's smack in the middle of the other lots. I'm afraid I made a mistake in buying the other property before getting Miss Blessing's agreement, but I was afraid word would get out about the railroad and prices would go up beyond what we could afford. If that happened, we'd be in worse shape than we are now."

Prescott closed his eyes for a moment. Had he come

all this way to fail? He set his jaw. No. He *wasn't* going to fail.

He met Walt's gaze. "What's the woman's reason for not selling?"

"I don't know. I made her a good offer. The best one of all because there's a house and a deep well on the land. Of course, we'll tear down the house, but having that well would save us plenty before we're through. But she won't even talk about selling." He shook his head. "I'm sorry, Prescott. I'd hoped to have the matter cleared up before you got here."

"Maybe she's holding out, thinking we'll pay her more than the land's worth."

"I don't think so. She doesn't seem the type. Keeps to herself most of the time. Except for Sundays when she goes to church or when she delivers her sewing to the dress shop, I've hardly seen her leave that house of hers. I heard she was born there, and she must intend to die there, too."

Prescott rose to his feet, then turned and reached for his hat. "I think I'd better have a talk with this Miss—" He looked over his shoulder. "What did you say her name is?"

"Blessing. Felicity Blessing."

"Miss Felicity Blessing." He envisioned her—petite, white-haired, probably a little hard of hearing. Surely he could reason with her, help her see that selling her home and land would benefit her. He set his hat on his head. "I'll convince her to sell." He turned and walked toward the door.

"Good luck," Walt called after him, but the tone of his

voice said he didn't hold out much hope for Prescott's success.

———

ANGEL EMELINE SAT on the window ledge and stared out at the town. Why hadn't she obtained more information from Archie? Like who it was Felicity Blessing needed to find. She was convinced Archie had a particular human in mind. If she hadn't been in such a hurry to get here...

No doubt, Archie had noted her failure to do proper advance preparation, too. Nothing got by him. Nothing.

She glanced toward Felicity who sat in her straight-backed chair near the other window, sewing a blue dress. The color would have been splendid on Felicity, much better than the tan blouse and dull brown skirt she wore now. But, of course, the blue dress was for some other woman.

How was Angel Emeline to answer Felicity's prayers when the woman tried to convince herself she was content with her life as it was? It didn't take an angel to see she was lonely.

And that was why Angel Emeline was here. To help answer a secret prayer, a silent prayer that was heartfelt and true, even though not acknowledged.

Angel Emeline returned her gaze to the window, wondering again how best to help. Felicity made no efforts to change her life. She spent her days cleaning her little house and sewing dresses for other women. If she didn't want to be alone—if she wanted love, marriage and children—shouldn't she go where she might meet eligible men? Surely Felicity realized a man wasn't going to walk right up to her door and knock.

And that was the precise moment Angel Emeline saw the answer to Felicity's prayer stride into view.

Chapter 2

The knock on her door caused Felicity to look up in surprise. She rarely had visitors, especially in the middle of the day. She set aside the dress she was making for Mrs. Babcock's shop and rose from her chair. As she approached the door, Angel jumped down from the window sill to stand beside her.

"Who is it, pet?" Felicity opened the door.

"Miss Blessing?" the stranger asked, a hint of surprise in his voice.

He was tall—a good six inches taller than Felicity—with hair the color of ink, intense blue eyes, and chiseled features. Her heart skipped a beat at the sight of him. He held a dusty Stetson in one hand, and his clothes bore evidence of travel, yet he didn't look unkept.

"Miss *Felicity* Blessing?"

"Yes. I'm Felicity Blessing. May I help you?"

Here's a man you could love. Her pulse quickened at

the unexpected thought, and she felt her skin grow flushed.

"My name's Prescott Jones. I'm Walt Johnson's business partner. I'd like to speak with you a moment if I may."

Felicity felt a sting of disappointment. "If it's about selling my home, Mr. Jones, you're wasting your time."

Angel darted out the door and wound her way around the visitor's legs, meowing for attention.

Prescott grinned as he reached down and picked up the cat with one hand. "Seems your cat's willing to listen." He met Felicity's gaze, still smiling. "Won't you at least give me an opportunity to speak to you?"

Listen to what he has to say, Felicity. What can it hurt?

She felt that odd hiccup in her chest again. Almost of its own volition, her hand widened the opening. "I suppose it wouldn't hurt to listen, Mr. Jones. Please come in."

He entered, and as he walked past her, she was amazed at how small she felt beside him. She was self-conscious about her unusual height. Hard not to be when she towered over all the women in town—and a good many of the men as well.

"Please make yourself comfortable," she said.

Still holding the cat with one arm, Prescott sat on the sofa and placed his hat on the cushion beside him. Angel purred loudly as she rubbed her head against his chest. The action surprised Felicity. Her cat was normally stand-offish. But not with Mr. Jones.

Lucky cat.

She blushed, surprised by the image that popped into her head. The image of her cheek pressed against that chest. What in heaven's name was the matter with her? Tilting her chin, she said, "Please don't feel you have to spoil Angel by holding her."

"I like cats. Seems Angel likes me, too."

You wouldn't be lonely with a man like him around. He's got shoulders a woman could lean on.

Where on earth were these outrageous thoughts coming from? And how could she silence them? "You wished to speak to me about Mr. Johnson's offer?"

Prescott's smile faded. "Yes. Miss Blessing, I'm sure Walt told you how we intend to use the property. A cannery would mean employment for many people in Appleton, and it would mean increased profits for the farmers hereabouts." He leaned forward, his forearms resting on his thighs but still careful not to squish the cat. His eyes were bright with enthusiasm. "It could even mean the railroad would bring a spur up this way. That would benefit everyone who finds it necessary to travel as well as those shipping to market."

"But there must be other land—"

"Not as perfect as this site. Close to town. Close to the orchards. Right on the main road. Not far from the river."

She glanced down at her hands. "This is my home, Mr. Jones."

"You could have a better one."

"This house ... it's the one thing I can leave to you

when I die, Felicity." Her mother's voice echoed in her mind. *"Don't sell it. Don't leave it unless you leave it for love. And don't ever let your pa take you away from here. This is your home. You remember that."*

She did remember. She tried always to remember what her mother had told her.

———

PRESCOTT SAW a look of pain flit across Felicity's face. It was not a beautiful face. It was too long and narrow for that, and her brown eyes were too widely spaced, her mouth too full and generous. A plain face, perhaps, but not unpleasant. Her thick brown hair was worn in a bun, and he couldn't help wondering what she might look like with it loose and soft about her shoulders.

He also wondered why she seemed determined to remain in this cramped house when accepting his offer could provide her with something better. Her home was unremarkable in any fashion. It had no more than three rooms—the sitting room, a kitchen and a bedroom. She could own something better, if only she'd listen to reason.

Felicity looked up, the sadness still present in her eyes. "I can't sell, Mr. Jones. Not for any price."

"Do you realize we've purchased the land surrounding yours?"

She shook her head.

"We're going to build a factory, Miss Blessing. If you don't sell to us, you'll find yourself living in the middle of it."

Her eyes widened.

He set the cat on the floor and rose from the sofa, hat in hand. "We've no other choice."

"But, Mr. Jones, surely you can't mean—"

"I'm afraid I do."

Her face went as white as chalk. "I suppose you must do as your conscience guides."

"Yes, that's exactly what I'll do."

She said nothing more nor did she stand to show him to the door. She remained in her chair, back stiff, head high, with only a slight quiver in the corners of her mouth revealing her emotions.

Prescott strode out of the house before he could say something he'd regret. And if she was upset, it was her own fault. Did she think the threat of a few tears would change his mind?

Long, determined strides carried him back into town.

The woman needed to understand how important this factory was to the people of Appleton. Didn't she care about the rest of the community? Was she so self-centered she gave no thought to others? His pace slowed as he remembered Felicity's expression as he'd left her house. Self-centered? No. He thought frightened and uncertain described her better.

He felt a twinge of guilt but shoved it aside. He'd come to Appleton to build his factory and settle down. From the moment he'd read Walt's letter, the one telling him of the town's need for a cannery, Prescott had known his days of wandering were over. He was going to find everything he'd ever wanted here—a business, a home, a wife and family. He believed it with an unshakable certainty.

And Miss Felicity Blessing was not going to keep him from it.

FELICITY STARED at the door long after it had swung shut behind her unexpected visitor. Her heart still beat erratically in her chest, and try as she might to tell herself it was because of his threat to build his factory around her house, she wasn't fooled. It was the man himself who'd caused her pulse to race.

This time it was her father's voice that taunted her. *"Don't waste your time wantin' what you can't have, daughter. The men hereabouts won't take you to wife except out of desperation. Just like I took your ma. You listen to me now, Felicity. I'm tellin' you this for your own good."*

What he'd said was true. No man had ever looked at her unless he was certain there was no one else available. No one had wanted to love her. She'd seen it happen with her own eyes, felt it happen with her own heart.

She exhaled through her nose and reached for her sewing. She wasn't going to feel sorry for herself. She wasn't! But before she could pick up the fabric, Angel jumped into her lap, purring loudly.

"Traitor," she muttered, remembering the way the cat had warmed to their visitor.

Angel rubbed the top of her head against Felicity's chin, and suddenly Felicity couldn't bear the hollow ache any longer. Gathering the cat close to her, she pressed her face against the soft, white fur and wept.

Chapter 3

*W*alt opened the door to his two-story house and ushered Prescott inside. "Rebecca?" he called, and a moment later, a petite blond woman appeared at the top of the stairs. "Rebecca, this is my good friend, Prescott Jones."

Prescott watched as Walt's wife gracefully descended the stairs, her hand extended in warm welcome. "Mr. Jones, you cannot imagine how pleased I am to meet you at last. For years, I've listened to stories of your boyhood escapades with my husband." Her eyes twinkled with amusement. "I'll be most interested to hear your versions." She paused, still smiling, then added, "You are most welcome in our home."

"Thank you," he answered as he took hold of her hand.

Walt hadn't exaggerated. Rebecca Millard Johnson was an extraordinary beauty. If her sister was even half as lovely, Prescott would consider himself lucky.

It had been Walt's last letter that had finally made up Prescott's mind about moving to Idaho.

> ... Rebecca's sister will be visiting us for the entire summer. Charlotte is as beautiful as my darling wife. If she's like Rebecca in other ways, any man would be lucky to gain her affections. Certainly my wife has been a blessing and helpmeet to me. She makes my home a place of joy and comfort and is a good companion at all times. Could her sister, raised by the same parents, be any different?
>
> Come to Appleton, Prescott, and meet her. Perhaps, if you do, we shall be family one day. If you were to marry Charlotte, I could truly call you brother.

And so, here he was, hoping Charlotte would, indeed, be like her sister.

"We weren't expecting you for another week." Rebecca cast her husband a reproving glance. "I'll need some time to prepare your room. Why don't you and Walt sit in the parlor while I get things ready?"

"Don't go to any trouble for me. I—"

"Nonsense. It's no trouble at all." With a smile toward Prescott and another gently scolding frown at Walt, she went up the stairs and disappeared into a room near the top of the landing.

Walt clapped a hand on Prescott's shoulder. "Come on. We'd better do as she says." Wearing an amused grin, he turned and led the way down the hall. "I've learned it's wise never to argue with Rebecca. She finds the most interesting ways to have retribution if I do." A chuckle belied the ominous sound of his words.

Prescott followed Walt into a spacious parlor. The room had large windows which let in the late May sunlight. The sofa and chairs were upholstered in bright florals that matched the window draperies. The fireplace mantel and tables were covered with china figurines and lamps with tasseled shades. It was a room that bespoke of its master's success and its mistress's penchant for knickknacks.

For some inexplicable reason, he thought of Felicity Blessing's sitting room — plain, simple, tiny — and found it more to his liking than this more elaborate one.

"Sit down, Prescott," Walt urged. "How about something to drink? I've got an excellent brandy."

He shook his head. "No thanks." He wandered across the room and glanced out the window.

The yard behind the house was cluttered with signs of children — a ball and bat, a swing tied to the branches of a tall tree, a couple of dolls. Not far beyond were fruit orchards, and beyond them, a stark, gray-brown bluff signaled the course of a winding river. In the distance, wrapped in the haze of afternoon, a purple mountain range rippled across the horizon, the peaks still dusted with snow.

"You haven't told me what reason Miss Blessing gave you for refusing our offer," Walt said, his words accompanied by the splash of brandy being poured into a glass.

Prescott envisioned Felicity, sitting stiffly in her straight-backed chair. "She didn't give me one. Just said she couldn't sell."

"Are you really going to build the cannery around her house?"

He turned from the window. "I don't have any other choice. Too much money is tied up in that land. Unless you've got unlimited funds." He watched the other man shake his head. "Neither do I. So I guess that means we proceed as planned."

Walt lifted his glass in a salute. "To the J&J Canning Company."

"To our success," Prescott added, determined it would come true.

FELICITY SAT at her small table and stared at the food she'd prepared for her supper. The simple fare looked unappetizing, not because it wasn't good but because she wasn't hungry. She couldn't get thoughts of Prescott Jones out of her head.

She set her fork on the table and folded her hands in her lap, clenching them tightly.

It was only because of his threat. That was the reason for her distress. It was only because he *could* build his

factory around her, as he'd threatened, and she was help-
less to stop him.

Yet it wasn't his warning she remembered. She kept
seeing him standing in her doorway, towering above her,
his shoulders broad, his body lean and strong. She envisioned the ink-black hair, shaggy around the collar of his
shirt, the slight cleft in his chin, the straight line of his
dark eyebrows above startling blue eyes.

She shook her head, trying to dislodge his image from
her mind.

Suddenly, Angel jumped up on the chair opposite
her.

"Get down," Felicity ordered, surprised by the cat's
actions. "You know better than that. What's the matter
with you?"

Angel simply stared at her.

*When was the last time a man was in your home,
Felicity?*

Her breath caught in her chest.

It was nice to have him here, wasn't it?

She forgot the cat sitting at the table, wanting only to
rid herself of the unwelcome questions she could hear so
clearly in her head, so clearly Felicity could have sworn
there was someone in the room asking them of her.

You liked his smile, didn't you?

A tiny groan escaped her throat as she rose from the
chair and walked into the sitting room.

Maybe he'll come back.

Her pulse quickened.

"Maybe he'll come back," she whispered, realizing she hoped he would and was dismayed because of it.

REBECCA'S SISTER joined them for supper, and she was as beautiful as Prescott had been told. Charlotte Millard, all of twenty-years-old, had the same silver-blond hair, the same delicate features, and the same slender figure as her older sister. She even had the same warm smile.

As the four adults sat around the table, enjoying the best meal Prescott had eaten in the better part of a year, Charlotte listened to every word that came out of his mouth as if they'd been dipped in gold. She laughed often and told Prescott he was tremendously amusing. She asked him questions about himself, about his work, about his travels.

"Of course, I've only been in Appleton a short while myself, but I think you're going to like it here," she said in her wispy voice. "I almost wish I didn't have to return to Seattle at the end of summer."

Prescott thought Charlotte was the sort of girl most men would dream of marrying. The bachelors of Appleton would be buzzing around her door all summer long. If she wanted a husband, she would have one easily enough. "Perhaps you'll decide not to leave, Miss Millard."

Charlotte smiled before looking down, long lashes

brushing her cheeks. "Does that mean you hope I'll stay, Mr. Jones?"

"Charlotte," Rebecca admonished.

He would have answered affirmatively if he'd had the opportunity.

"Reow."

Everyone turned toward the open dining room window to find a white cat perched on the sill.

"For heaven's sake," Rebecca said. "Where on earth did he come from?"

"She," Prescott interjected. "That's Miss Blessing's cat. Angel. Angel and I became acquainted earlier today." He rose from his chair and walked toward the window. "What are you doing this far from home, kitty?"

Angel leapt into his arms as he reached to pick her up.

He turned toward the others. "Friendly, isn't she?" He stroked Angel's head.

Charlotte held a handkerchief up to her nose and sneezed. Once, then again and again. When she could catch her breath, she waved her handkerchief in Prescott's direction. "It's the cat. They make me sneeze." She gulped several quick breaths of air, her nose wrinkled. "Oh, do put that dreadful beast outside where ... where ... where it be—belongs." She finished with a string of sneezes.

You'd better take her back to Miss Blessing. A wagon could hit her in the dark. You wouldn't want that to happen.

"I'd better take her back to Miss Blessing," he said,

echoing the small voice he'd heard in his head. "I won't be long."

He left the house to the sounds of Charlotte's sneezing.

Outside, the air was sweet with the smell of blossoming spring flowers. Night had settled over the earth, bringing with it the singing of crickets and chirping of frogs. Yellow lamplight spilled from windows to form an uneven checkerboard pattern along the main street of town.

She's not really your sort, that Charlotte Millard.

Prescott's pace slowed, and a frown furrowed his brow.

Why would he think such a thing? A man would be lucky to have a wife like Charlotte. True, she was seventeen years his junior but that didn't seem to trouble her so he didn't see why it should be a problem.

She doesn't like cats. She thinks they're dreadful beasts.

True, but how could he fault her for that? She couldn't help it if they made her sneeze. Charlotte seemed sweet-natured and was obviously eager to please, and there was no denying she was pretty to look at. What more could a man want in a wife?

Intelligence, for one. A kind heart, for another. What about Miss Blessing?

He nearly laughed out loud. Miss Blessing? Now there was a woman who wasn't his sort. She was a stubborn, stiff-lipped old maid. And plain-looking to boot. She couldn't hold a candle to Charlotte.

With more determined steps, he left the light of town

behind, his way now guided by the full moon rising at his back.

He intended to leave the cat on the stoop without disturbing her mistress, but just as he drew close to the house, the front door opened and Felicity Blessing stepped outside. Moonlight caused her white wrapper to glow. Dark hair spilled over her shoulders and down her back. Apparently, she'd been preparing for bed.

"Angel?" she called softly.

"She's here, Miss Blessing."

He heard her gasp, saw her hand flutter to her chest as her eyes found him.

"Sorry. I didn't mean to startle you." He drew closer. "Your cat wandered into town. I brought her back."

Felicity held out her arms to take Angel from him. "I don't know what's gotten into her. She's never run off before."

Prescott gave her the cat, saw the gentle way she cradled the animal.

"Thank you, Mr. Jones."

The moonlight had softened her features, making her seem less stiff and formidable. He'd been right about her hair, too. It was beautiful, cascading over her shoulders instead of pulled so harshly back from her face.

"It was kind of you to bring her back."

"Glad to do it, Miss Blessing."

"I ... I wouldn't want to lose her."

You ought to kiss her.

He cleared his throat, surprised by the wayward

thought, and took a step backward. "Well, I'd better get back to the Johnson house. Good night, Miss Blessing."

"Good night, Mr. Jones. And thank you again."

Her voice lingered in his head long after he'd left her little house behind him.

Chapter 4

*P*rescott was out at his property just after dawn the next morning. With precise steps, he walked off the perimeter of the main factory building, marking the corners with stakes. Of course, the U-shape was a bit odd, but it wouldn't be too great an inconvenience for the workers.

And if Miss Felicity Blessing wanted to live smack-dab in the middle of a canning factory, that was her decision, not his.

He paused and glanced toward the house, wondering again about the woman inside—and wondering why he continued to think about her. Last night he'd been unable to shake the memory of her standing in the moonlight. Even being in Charlotte's company hadn't driven Felicity's image from his mind.

As if in answer to his thoughts, the back door of the tiny house opened and Felicity stepped outside, carrying a pail as she walked toward the pump at a rear corner of the house.

Look at that. The place isn't even plumbed into the kitchen. Why does she want to hold onto it when she could have better?

That thought was fleeting, replaced by another. Her hair was still down, and it was even more lovely by daylight. It flowed like a dark waterfall over her shoulders and down her back, a stark contrast to her simple white wrapper. The luxurious mahogany strands glowed in the sun, reflecting hints of gold amidst the umber.

At that moment, Angel ran out the open back door and headed straight toward him. Felicity's gaze followed the cat, and when she discovered Prescott watching her, her cheeks turned scarlet and her hand stilled on the pump handle.

He touched the brim of his hat. "Good morning."

She nodded and pushed her loose hair over her shoulder with one hand.

"I thought I'd better get an early start." He motioned toward the stakes.

The blush paled.

He rubbed his chin as he considered what he should do, then strode toward her with purposeful steps. "Miss Blessing."

She clutched the front of her wrapper with one hand and pressed her body back against the side of the house, looking for all the world as if she expected him to assault her on the spot.

He stopped, irritation flaring. "Miss Blessing, isn't it

time we tried to find a solution to this problem? If we could just talk—"

"Talk would not change my mind, Mr. Jones. I can't sell my home." She gripped the handle of the pail with both hands and hurried toward the house, her head tipped forward and her eyes downcast.

Stubborn woman! Why on earth wouldn't she listen to reason? Why was she being so difficult?

She's afraid.

Afraid. Yes. That seemed to be true. But what had she to be afraid of?

Felicity stopped in the back doorway and looked over her shoulder in his direction. He thought for a moment she'd changed her mind, that she would say they could talk about it after all. But she didn't.

"Angel. Come inside, pet. Come here, kitty."

She needs a friend.

He glanced down at the cat near his feet. As crazy as it sounded, Angel's green eyes seemed to offer an apology for Felicity's behavior and beg him to be understanding. Then the feline dashed after her mistress.

Prescott shook his head. Fanciful thinking and very unlike him.

He saw Felicity close the door behind her.

What does she have to be afraid of? He wasn't trying to turn her out into the street. She needn't leave Appleton and her neighbors. She could live right in town but in a nicer place. She could have a bigger house with water plumbed into the kitchen. Her refusal made no sense. It wasn't the least bit logical.

Prescott shook his head again. If Felicity Blessing needed a friend, she was going about it the wrong way as far as he was concerned.

With that, he turned and continued walking off the perimeters of the factory, hammering stakes into the ground as he went.

FELICITY SAT ON A KITCHEN CHAIR, her hands shaking, her breathing rapid. She kept remembering the way she'd felt as Prescott Jones stepped toward her, the way her knees threatened to buckle, the way her mouth went dry, the way her body tingled with sensations both wonderful and terrifying. If she closed her eyes, she could still see him. And he would be outside her door every day, building his factory and then running it.

Why wouldn't she sell her house as he wanted? His offer was fair. More than fair even. But she couldn't sell. She'd made a promise to her mother.

"Don't ever sell the house, Felicity. No matter what happens, don't ever sell it unless it's because you've found real love. Promise me."

"Oh, Mama."

She pictured Naomi Blessing, the day she'd spoken those words. Her mother, worn down by time and her father's ever-present disapproval and harsh words. Her mother, lying in her bed, the promise of death written in her feverish eyes as she held her young daughter's hand.

"I was so lonely, Felicity. I didn't care that he didn't

love me. But I was wrong. I should have cared. I was better off alone. Except for you, of course."

Felicity remembered the feel of her mother's fingertips as they'd brushed her cheek.

"If he'd ever loved me, he could have had so much."

"I love you, Mama," she whispered now, just as she had then.

"All the riches Sam has ever wanted were here, waiting for him. It's all right here. Don't you do what I did. Don't you ever settle for less than love. Not even for children."

With a sigh, Felicity rose from the chair, one hand pushing her hair over her shoulder at the same time she pushed away the old memories. She had no time to dwell upon the past. She must wash and dress and get on with her day. She needed to deliver the blue dress to Mrs. Babcock before noon, and there was her weekly laundry to wash and her mending to do.

But before Felicity left the kitchen, she was drawn to the window where she peered around the edges of the curtains, just enough to find Prescott as he moved a few stakes, modifying the configuration of his canning factory. He walked from one stake to another with a long, easy stride, the stride of a man with confidence in who he was and what he was doing. A man unafraid to go after what he wanted.

"Always wanting what you weren't meant to have, aren't you, girl?" Her father's voice, full of scorn. *"Your ma filled your head with nonsense."*

She turned her back to the window.

Her father had been right. Long ago, Felicity had wanted things she couldn't have. But over the years, she'd stopped wanting, stopped hoping for the impossible. She'd learned to be content with her life the way it was.

Angel brushed up against the hem of her skirt, her purr extra loud in the small kitchen. Felicity glanced down at the cat. Angel watched her as if she knew what Felicity had been thinking.

Who says you can't have what you want?

"I'm fine, Angel. I like things as they are."

Squaring her shoulders, Felicity left the kitchen and performed her morning ablutions, finishing them by smoothing her hair back from her face and winding it into a tight bun at her nape. Afterward, she prepared her breakfast without ever once returning to the window to see if Prescott Jones was still in the field outside.

When her meal was finished and the dishes properly washed, dried and put away, she put on her bonnet, picked up the blue gown she'd finished late last night, and left the house, her head held high, certain she had banished thoughts about a certain newcomer to Appleton.

PRESCOTT STEPPED out of Walt's office in time to see Felicity Blessing walking along the boardwalk, coming toward him. Everything about her was stiff, from the straightness of her back to the firm line of her mouth. He saw nothing of the woman in a flowing white wrapper whom he'd glimpsed last night and again this morning.

She looked up and saw him, and her pace faltered. Then he saw the proud tilt of her chin as she proceeded forward. His own stubborn streak asserted itself, keeping him right where he was, in the middle of her path.

"Good morning again, Miss Blessing." He bent his hat brim and gave her a smile.

She was forced to stop. "Mr. Jones."

She was tall for a woman, making it easier to look her directly in the eyes. Her eyes were chocolate brown, and behind them, he saw something. Something softer, more vulnerable. And she would detest that he saw it.

"Prescott!"

He stepped back from Felicity and turned in the direction of Charlotte's voice, annoyed by her use of his Christian name. Though the reason for his annoyance, he couldn't say. He watched the young woman cross the street, her sunshine-bright smile all for him.

"Oh, I'm so glad I found you here." She stepped onto the boardwalk. "Rebecca decided we should have a picnic by the river. Do say you'll join us. I would be devastated if you weren't there."

"Well, I—"

She turned toward Felicity. "Good morning, ma'am. I'm sorry if I interrupted, but I was so excited to have found Prescott, I completely forgot my manners. Please do forgive me."

"Of course," Felicity replied softly.

Charlotte slipped her hand into the crook of

Prescott's arm but kept her gaze on Felicity. "Isn't it exciting about Prescott's plans? He told me all about the cannery last night at supper. I know he's going to have wonderful success." She glanced up at him. "The whole town will be indebted to him and my brother-in-law."

Felicity's gaze moved from Charlotte to Prescott. "I'm sure many will feel indebted."

Prescott could almost hear Felicity adding: *I am not one of them.*

Felicity took a step forward. "Please excuse me. I must deliver this dress to Mrs. Babcock."

Prescott had no choice but to step out of her way, drawing Charlotte with him. He wasn't even sure why he'd tried to keep her there in the first place.

Charlotte's fingers on his arm drew his attention back to her. "Do say you'll come with us on our picnic."

She was pretty and warm and full of promise. She was exactly the sort of woman he'd had in mind for a wife. Thanks to Walt's words of praise for his sister-in-law, Charlotte was one of the reasons Prescott had come to Appleton. Nothing had happened to change that. He needed to remember it.

"I'll come," he replied while resisting the urge to turn and catch one last glimpse of Felicity.

SOLVING a human's problems was not as simple as Angel Emeline had expected. Still, she was making a bit of progress. Prescott Jones was obviously the answer to

Felicity Blessing's prayers. Equally obvious to Angel Emeline was the woman's attraction to him. Time, she supposed, was all that was needed now. Time and her continued suggestions to Felicity and Prescott.

If she was able to handle this assignment without asking Archie for assistance, her promotion to Angel, Second Grade, would be in the bag. Since these two people were right for each other, how could anything go wrong now?

Angel Emeline rose from her place on the floor and stretched before pattering across the sitting room and jumping up onto the window ledge. She sat down and allowed her long tail to wrap around her paws, enjoying the silky feel of it.

She turned her gaze out the window, and as if on cue, a buggy appeared on the road, carrying two couples in the direction of the river. Prescott was included in the merry party. So was that sneezing Charlotte Millard.

Hmmm. There's what could go wrong.

It seemed Angel Emeline was going to have to do a little more than make mental suggestions to Felicity and Prescott. And judging by the attractive young woman seated beside Prescott in that buggy, Angel needed to act quickly.

But what exactly was she to do? How could she bring Felicity and Prescott together where they belonged?

As the buggy passed by the little house, an idea sprang to mind. Now, if she could just get the timing right.

Chapter 5

*P*rescott pulled the team of horses to a halt at the far end of the factory property. Drawing the heavy leather reins from around his neck and looping them to the plow, he turned to view his handiwork.

The past two days had been spent clearing and leveling the land. He'd done this part of the work himself, but when construction began on the cannery, he would need to hire plenty of other laborers. And it wouldn't be long until then. In fact, he expected a load of lumber to be delivered to the site today.

He couldn't resist a satisfied grin. The J&J Canning Company would be a reality by midsummer. From all appearances, the fruit crop would be a healthy one, which would mean the cannery would be busy come harvest. It seemed the years of scraping by, making do, scrimping and saving and investing were about to pay off.

And if Walt and Rebecca Johnson had anything to say about it, Prescott would be engaged by September.

Their pleasure in seeing Prescott and Charlotte together was unmistakable, and it seemed Charlotte was willing to marry him. She watched him with an adoring expression whenever they were together. *Sometimes a bit too adoring*, he thought, then told himself he was wrong. After all, how could a woman be too adoring?

For his part, it was rather early to feel anything akin to love or to bring up the subject of matrimony, but he expected both would happen, given time. What wasn't to love about Charlotte? He only had to look at Walt and Rebecca and their children to see what his future with her would be like. It was what he wanted. Wasn't it?

His gaze strayed to the little house in the midst of his property.

He hadn't seen Felicity in the past two days, not since their encounter on the boardwalk outside Walt's office. He wondered if she'd given more thought to selling her house. She had to be aware of the work he'd done out here. She had to have seen the stakes in the ground and visualized the u-shaped factory surrounding three sides of her home. When the lumber came and the actual building began, surely she wouldn't want to remain.

Maybe he should talk to her again. Try one more time to change her mind.

He wiped his forehead with his shirtsleeve and raked his fingers through his hair in an effort to look more presentable before walking toward the house. He was nearly there when he saw the lumber wagon coming down the road from town. He raised his arm and hailed

the driver. The driver slapped the reins against the back-
sides of the team of horses, quickening their pace.

Prescott wasn't aware of the door of Felicity's house
opening, not until he saw a blur of white fur dart out into
the road, right into the path of the team of horses. Behind
him came a woman's scream. The horses squealed as the
driver yanked hard on the reins. The team reared back in
their traces. Felicity hurried toward the road, skirts and
petticoats flying. Prescott followed an instant later. The
wagon finally stopped.

Prescott reached Angel first. The white cat was limp
and still, one leg lying at an odd angle. He feared the
feline might be dead.

"Angel?" Felicity knelt on the dirt road beside
Prescott. She reached out and lightly touched the cat,
then drew her hand back and clutched it to her chest.

The cat didn't stir.

Felicity glanced up at Prescott, and he found the look
in her eyes unbearable. After a moment, he had to look
away. He held his finger against Angel's throat, thankful
to find a pulse. It was weak but it was there. "She's still
alive, Miss Blessing. Does Appleton have a vet? We need
to stop the bleeding."

"No. There's no vet."

"What about the doctor? Will he treat animals?"

"He's gone to the capital city to visit his son."

"Well, I'll see what I can do for her, then." He slid his
hands beneath Angel and gently lifted her off the ground.

Felicity led the way into the house. She directed

Prescott into the bedroom and motioned for him to lay the cat on the bed.

"I'll need some water, scissors, and a needle and thread." He examined the wound. "And some bandages and a splint of some sort."

"I'll get it for you."

After Felicity returned with the requested items, Prescott trimmed away the hair from the wound and cleansed the gash, then sewed it closed. He bound the cat's torso with strips of white cloth, then wrapped her front left leg with care, hoping, if she survived, that she wouldn't be crippled. Angel didn't move or protest throughout the process, but Prescott thought her pulse seemed stronger when he checked it.

"Where did you learn to do that?" Felicity asked as he washed his hands in the basin near the bed.

He met her gaze. "Practice."

She waited, her silence encouraging him to continue.

"I had a cat of my own when I was a boy." That was stretching the truth, of course. The orphanage hadn't allowed pets. "I called him Scrapper 'cause he was always getting into fights." He shrugged. "I sewed him up a time or two."

She stroked the cat's head. "You may have saved Angel's life."

He started to deny it.

"If you hadn't been here, I couldn't have helped her. She might have died. How can I ever thank you?"

He almost suggested she could thank him by selling her house, but the look in her eyes stopped him. It was like he could see into her heart. He understood her, understood why she couldn't bear the thought of losing Angel. Because the cat was all she had. That had been true of him and Scrapper, too.

Felicity looked away.

"Well." He stepped toward the bedroom doorway. "I guess I'd better see to my lumber. The driver's probably anxious to be on his way, and I've got a lot of work to get done." He paused, then added, "I'll check back this afternoon. If that's all right?"

"Yes. Thank you. Please do."

———

FELICITY KNELT beside the bed and continued stroking Angel's head. "You'll be all right. Mr. Jones took good care of you."

He'd take good care of you, too, if you'd give him a chance.

She remembered Prescott's strong but gentle hands as they'd tended the injured animal.

He understands about being lonely.

Now, why would she think that? She didn't know anything about him.

Why don't you do something different with your hair? Prescott would like it down. Take it down.

She rose from her knees and walked to the mirror hanging on the wall. Staring at her reflection, she wondered if a man like Prescott Jones would notice any changes she made to her appearance. And why would he? Judging by the young and very lovely Miss Millard, he was not free to notice such things about Felicity.

She turned away from the mirror and began removing her hairpins.

Don't give up without trying, Felicity!

She had gone beyond being an eccentric old maid. She'd gone completely mad. It was one thing to talk to her cat. It was entirely another to hear voices in her head —and then do what they told her to do! And yet she didn't stop what she was doing until her hair was free of pins. Then she picked up her brush and began stroking it down the length of her hair. The slow motion of her hand and the gentle tugging at her scalp was somehow soothing.

Closing her eyes, her thoughts drifted back to a happier time when life had seemed simple, joyful, full of promise. She gazed into the past and saw her mother in a chair near the fire. As Naomi Jones brushed Felicity's hair, she'd shared stories about Felicity's maternal grand-parents, about how they'd come west, about how Grandpa Greer had built their first shelter — just a hut, really — from the cottonwoods that grew near the river, about how he'd planted the saplings he'd brought with him from the family fruit orchards back in New York. She'd told Felicity how they were alone for so long when Naomi was a child, about how Grandma Greer had schooled Naomi, just as Naomi had schooled Felicity, teaching her to read and write and do her sums. She remembered the way her mother had stroked her head and told her she was going to grow up to be pretty and smart, how she was going to marry a man who would treasure her.

The remembrance slowly changed. The new image in her mind was quite different from her favorite childhood memories. She imagined Prescott Jones standing behind her, brushing her hair, one large hand on her shoulder. She imagined him standing so close she could feel the heat of his body upon her skin. She imagined him leaning down and kissing the crown of her head. She imagined—

Her eyes flew open, and she looked at her reflection in the mirror. Her face was flushed, her eyes bright and wide. Her hair fell in waves around her shoulders, the ends curling softly.

"Ohhh." The word came out on a whisper of air as she twisted her hair quickly into a bun and jabbed the pins into place, then turned away from the mirror before any other unwelcome images could spring to mind.

IT WAS a good thing cats purportedly had nine lives, Angel Emeline thought as she lay on the bed, aching all over. She obviously had used up one for this poor animal.

Her timing was abysmal. She hadn't meant to actually run beneath that dreadful horse's hooves. She'd meant to make it look as if she'd been hurt. But she hadn't failed completely. Prescott had said he would come back in the afternoon. One more chance to bring these two souls together.

Chapter 6

*A*s he worked, the afternoon sun beat upon Prescott's back, and the earth threw the heat up into his face. Not a single cloud marred the vast expanse of blue sky. There would be no temporary respite from the glare.

Sweat had left darkened patches on Prescott's shirt, and he felt the grit on his skin. But he only had one more row to drag and then he'd be finished for the day. Tomorrow he would start hiring his construction crew.

Clucking to the horses, he guided the team in a tight turn. He was just about to smack the reins against their rumps when he saw Felicity Blessing approaching him, bucket in hand.

She stopped near the horses. "I thought you might be thirsty, Mr. Jones. It's unusually hot for this time of year." She held the bucket toward him. "Would you like a drink of water?"

He lifted the reins over his head. "'That's kind of you,

Miss Blessing."

"It's the least I can do after what you did for Angel."

He lifted a dipper full of water from the bucket and drained it in several long gulps, then repeated the action two more times. The fourth time he raised the dipper above him and let it pour over his head. When he opened his eyes, water dripping off his hair, he found her smiling as she watched him.

She had an unbelievable smile. It touched not only the corners of her mouth but her eyes as well. He couldn't help grinning in return as he passed her the dipper, their fingers touching briefly in the exchange.

She took a small step backward, her smile already fading. "You're welcome to help yourself to the water whenever you like." She turned to leave.

"Listen," he said quickly, stopping her, "why don't I come have a look at Angel now? Give the team a rest." He pointed to the bucket. "Then I'll fill that up and give the horses a drink, if you don't mind."

"I don't mind."

"Good." He wished she would smile again. "Here." He reached out and took the bucket from her hands. "Let me carry that."

As they fell into step, Felicity said, "Angel's slept most of the day, but she drank a little cream a while ago."

"That's a good sign."

"Is it?"

"Yes." He opened the back door, then waited for her to lead the way into the house.

The kitchen was as small a room as he'd expected it

to be. There was barely enough space for the black cooking stove, the dry sink, an icebox, a small cupboard, and a table with two chairs. But it was neat and uncluttered, the same as the other two rooms of the house.

In the bedroom, only a few steps away from the sitting room and kitchen, he found Angel where he'd left her that morning. When he stroked the top of her head, she opened her eyes and meowed at him.

"Maybe you learned a lesson today." Prescott sat on the edge of the bed. "Do you think so?"

"Reow."

He checked the bandages. The one around the cat's chest was white which meant his stitches had held. No more bleeding. He wasn't as certain about what he'd done for Angel's leg, although there didn't seem to be much swelling.

Felicity sat on the edge of the bed opposite him. "My father hated cats. If they weren't mousers, then the only use for them was drowning."

He glanced up. *Your father was an idiot.*

"I never had a pet until Angel. She showed up at my door one night. It was pouring down rain and she was cold and half-starved. I couldn't leave her outside. And once she was in, she never left."

"That's the way cats are. They make their homes where they want. It's not up to us."

Her smile returned. "What about Scrapper? How did he come to live with you?"

"Scrapper didn't really live with me. He made the streets his home. But when he wanted company, he'd climb the tree outside my window and I'd let him in." He didn't say how glad he'd been to see that mangy-looking animal, how he'd hidden Scrapper beneath the covers on his cot and held him close, feeding him whatever scraps of food he'd managed to sneak up to his room.

"Did your parents know?"

"My parents were dead."

Her voice softened. "I'm sorry. I didn't know."

"No reason you should've known. Besides, it was a long time ago."

"My mother died when I was twelve. My father passed on last year."

He hadn't talked about his family in years, but there was something about her tone of voice, about the way she watched him with her dark brown eyes, that made him want to confide in her. "I was six. The youngest son. I had three older brothers and two younger sisters. It was a fire that took them and my parents. I still don't know how I got out alive and the others didn't. I just remember wandering around outside in the middle of the night with the fire lighting up the sky."

"How tragic."

The worst part for Prescott was that he could no longer remember what any of them had looked like. He hadn't been able to keep their images in his mind, no matter how hard he tried. Sometimes he thought he heard a woman's voice that sounded like his mother's or heard a laugh that reminded him of his father or he saw children playing in a schoolyard and it seemed that he had done the same thing with his brothers. But when he tried to recall their faces, he couldn't, and that saddened him.

But he still remembered the warmth that had filled their big, old farmhouse in Illinois. He remembered how happy he'd been, how often everyone had laughed. And he remembered the love. When he married, he wanted a home like that. He wanted a home filled with laughter and warmth. He'd wanted it for a long time. He'd been saving and working toward it for years.

"Where did you live after they died?" Felicity asked gently.

This memory was clear in every detail. "There wasn't any other family, so I was sent to an orphanage in Chicago." He remembered the massive brick building and the cold-hearted matron who ran the place. He remembered being lonely. He remembered being scared. "That's where I met Walt. Puny little kid with big glasses. We were thick as thieves for the year he was there. Then he was adopted and moved away from Chicago. We kept in touch over the years. I could always count on letters from Walt, no matter where he was, no matter where I was."

"You never left the orphanage?"

"Not 'til I was sixteen." He shrugged. "It wasn't so bad once Scrapper came around."

"When was that?"

"Not long after Walt moved away. He showed up one night in the tree outside my window, meowing and making a fuss until I let him in. Scrapper always seemed to be there when I needed a friend."

FELICITY ENVISIONED the small boy with his alley cat friend and felt her heart squeeze. She understood what he'd left unsaid, better than he would ever know. Or maybe he did know. There was something about the way Prescott looked at her sometimes that made her think he could see right inside her soul. Made her think he understood her.

"Well." He rose from the bed. "I'd better get back to the horses. There's a lot of work to be done, and I'm expected for dinner at the Johnsons'."

She remembered Rebecca Johnson's pretty, young sister for the second time today and suddenly felt foolish for sitting on the bed, exchanging memories with Prescott Jones. How ridiculous to think there was some sort of connection between them because of their cats.

Smoothing her skirt with both hands, Felicity stood and led the way to the kitchen door. She opened it and stepped outside. "Thank you again for looking after Angel."

"I'll stop by in the morning, see how she did through the night."

Again, she remembered Charlotte. "I don't want to put you out, Mr. Jones. I'm sure she's out of danger, and the doctor should be back tomorrow."

"It's no trouble. I'll be working out here anyway."

Her throat felt tight, too tight to speak, so she simply nodded, then watched as he walked away.

Chapter 7

*L*ying in her bed, Felicity watched as the first streaks of daylight moved across her ceiling. She had spent a restless night, her thoughts returning again and again to Prescott Jones. She kept seeing him as he'd poured that dipper of water over his head, kept remembering the play of his muscles beneath his shirt, the look of his sun-browned forearms as his fingers raked the wet hair back from his face. She kept hearing him talk about the orphanage and Scrapper. He'd said so little and yet so much.

And some time this morning, he would come knocking at her door again. He would come to check on Angel's progress. He would come into her house, into her bedroom. His piercing blue eyes would look at her, and he would smile, making her heart thump in that strange way.

She closed her eyes and rolled onto her side, trying not to imagine more, for her thoughts were far from what was proper for an unmarried woman. She didn't want to imagine what it would be like to have Prescott Jones kiss her, to have him hold her.

But she did imagine it.

She told herself he was a stranger, an outsider. He'd been in Appleton no more than four days. She, on the other hand, had been born in this little town. She could count on her fingers the number of times she had spoken to Prescott Jones. There was no reason for her to think about him, no reason to feel the way she did. She was nothing to him but an obstacle to a last plot of ground.

With an exasperated groan, she tossed aside the bedcovers and sat up, lowering her feet to the floor. Dawn had managed to overtake the bedroom by this time, and Felicity's gaze immediately found Angel, lying on the bed of blankets Felicity had made for her the night before.

Angel raised her head and meowed.

Felicity smiled, recognizing the familiar demand for food. "You are feeling better, aren't you, pet?" She stood and crossed the room, then knelt to stroke the cat. "Thank God I didn't lose you."

Angel purred her concurrence.

Felicity's heart lightened at the sound. "I'll get you some cream."

She rose and hurried into the kitchen. Opening the icebox, she noted the need for more ice as she removed a small pitcher of cream. She mentally counted the money she had hidden in the crock on top of the cupboard. She could afford to buy a block of ice today. The pink frock would be finished by Monday, and Mrs. Babcock was prompt to pay Felicity when she delivered the ordered gowns.

She poured a generous amount of cream into a saucer and carried it to the bedroom. Angel lapped the saucer clean in no time at all.

Shouldn't you get ready? Prescott will be here soon.

She pressed the heels of her hands over her ears, as if she could shut out her thoughts, but it was too late. Her pulse had quickened. Her mind already envisioned him again.

Put on something pretty. It can't hurt.

Couldn't hurt? It was crazy! She was an old maid, too tall, too thin, too plain. She hadn't anything to wear that could disguise that truth. She reached for a brown calico.

Not that one.

Her hand stopped in midair.

Wear the new green one.

Mad. She was undeniably, indisputably, stark-raving mad.

After donning the green dress, she brushed her hair and began to twist it into the bun she always wore.

No! He likes it down.

But she couldn't possibly know how Prescott Jones liked her hair. Why would he have noticed her hair, one way or the other? Still, instead of the hair pins, she selected the bronze combs—her mother's favorites—and used them to pull her hair back from her face at the sides, leaving it falling down her back.

"I look ridiculous," she muttered as she stared at her reflection. "I look like I'm trying to be a girl again."

She might have talked herself into pinning her hair after all if the knock hadn't sounded at her door at that moment. Heart pounding erratically, she went to answer it.

"Good morning, Felicity," Doc Gordon said as the door opened. "I understand your cat had an accident yesterday."

She stared at him dumbly, disappointment stealing her ability to speak.

"May I come in?"

"Of course. How did you know about Angel?"

"When I got back last night, I happened to meet Mr. Jones, and he asked if I would have a look at your cat this morning." He walked past her into the sitting room. "Mr. Jones was afraid he didn't set the cat's leg properly."

This was what she deserved for thinking Prescott might care what she wore or how she combed her hair. It proved how useless something like vanity was for a woman like her. False vanity, for she had nothing to be vain about.

Shoulders squared, she led the doctor into her bedroom.

PRESCOTT SLIPPED the worm onto the hook, then handed the fishing pole to Stanley Johnson. With a great flourish, the boy cast the line out into the river.

"My dad showed me how to do that," he said.

From behind them, Prescott heard Charlotte's gentle warning. "Suzanne, you stay back from that water."

Prescott reached out and took hold of the little girl's hand. "Aunt Charlotte's right. Let's go back to the blanket. We can watch your brother from there."

Suzanne grinned at him. "Up! Up!"

He laughed as he lifted her into his arms, then pivoted and strolled to the blanket where Charlotte sat, her yellow and white skirt spread around her, like a sunflower in full bloom.

Charlotte smiled as they approached. "Dear heaven, I don't know how Rebecca manages when all four children are at home. I can scarcely keep up with Suzanne."

He set the three-year-old on her feet. "She's a lively one, all right."

"Suzanne, you sit down and stay put for a while. Here. Aunt Charlotte brought you something to play with." Charlotte pulled a porcelain doll from the wicker basket. "You take care of her, or Aunt Charlotte will be very displeased with you."

Prescott settled onto the blanket, watching Stanley.

"Are you hungry?" Charlotte asked. "Would you like to eat now?"

What he wanted was to return to Appleton, but he answered in the affirmative. What else could he do? When Rebecca asked him to take her sister and two youngest children fishing this morning, he'd known he was being maneuvered into spending more time with Charlotte, but he hadn't protested. Of course, he hadn't expected time to crawl, either. Charlotte had little to talk about except for her well-to-do friends in Seattle and the wonderful dances and parties they gave. He'd attempted to introduce a few new topics of interest, but she simply asked him what his own thoughts were, deftly turning the conversation back to him. He wondered why that trait no longer seemed as flattering as it had the first night they met.

The truth was, he found Charlotte more than a little boring. To put it simply, she was a spoiled young woman with few interests beyond herself. Oh, she was well trained in the art of flattery, but it was superficial at best. *She* was superficial.

As he reclined, bracing himself on his elbows and forearms, he wondered what Felicity Blessing would have to say about such topics as Idaho giving women the right to vote the previous year or about what differences the railroad might mean to the people of Appleton. Plenty. He was convinced of it. There was a woman who had her own opinions. If nothing else, he'd like to ask her how her cat was faring after being attended to by the physician.

"What are you thinking about, Prescott? You haven't heard a word I've said."

He blinked, then looked at Charlotte. "Oh, I was just wondering about Angel."

"Angel?"

"Miss Blessing's cat. I hope the doctor was able to take a look at her."

"Oh, that dreadful animal." She shook her head, her golden hair whispering over her shoulders. "I cannot imagine anyone making such a fuss over a cat."

"Miss Blessing's cat is rather special."

"I suppose that must be true if you've taken such a liking to it. Still, I couldn't bear one of those creatures in my home. I nearly start sneezing just thinking about it." She giggled, a lyrical sound that drifted away on the breeze. Her smile was fetching as she leaned toward him.

Prescott looked at her for several heartbeats, wondering why he didn't feel any desire to kiss her, especially when she so obviously wanted him to. Any man who wouldn't grab such an opportunity must be an idiot.

Then he was an idiot. He didn't intend to kiss her.

He stood. "I'd better help Stan with that pole if he's ever to catch a fish. I've still got a work crew to hire this afternoon." Then he walked away from Charlotte without a backward glance.

KNEELING on the kitchen floor in her oldest dress, Felicity scrubbed with a vengeance. She had discovered some years ago that a deep-down cleaning of the house helped her to think more clearly.

Dark strands of hair had worked free from her bun and clung to the moisture on her neck. Water splashed onto her bodice and skirt and left dark spots on the faded gray gown, but Felicity didn't care. She would look a whole sight worse before she finished scrubbing the house from one end to the other.

She was angered by her foolishness. For allowing her imagination to take flight. For thinking she might please

Prescott Jones with the way she wore her hair or by putting on a new gown. Why should he notice Felicity at all? And why should she want him to notice her? She was content with her life as it was.

Are you?

Yes, she was. Perfectly content.

She pressed harder on the scrub brush and tried not to think about the tall man with ink black hair and eyes the color of the Idaho sky, the orphan with a cat named Scrapper who, for a moment in time, had seemed to understand her as no one ever had.

Chapter 8

*a*lthough her house sparkled with its top-to-bottom cleaning, the work had done little to improve Felicity's state of mind. She scarcely heard a word the minister said during the church service the next morning, especially since she knew Prescott Jones and the entire Johnson family — including Miss Millard — were seated two pews behind her.

When the service was over, Felicity slipped away from the other worshippers, careful to avoid making eye contact with anyone. She had intended to go directly home, but for some reason, her feet carried her toward the apple orchards down the slope from her place. She walked slowly through the mature trees, enjoying the cool shade the leafy branches provided. She kept walking until she reached the last row of fruit trees. Then she sat down and stared at the winding river.

"Don't waste your time wantin' what you can't have, daughter."

She closed her eyes. Her father had been right. Wanting what she couldn't have only led to heartache. She was better off this way. Look how unhappy her mother had been.

"Miss Blessing?"

She gasped in surprise as she twisted to look behind her.

Prescott Jones drew closer. "I hope I'm not intruding."

Felicity shook her head.

"It's cooler here by the river." He sat beneath the neighboring tree. "How's Angel doing?"

"Very well, thank you." Her wretched heart pounded in her ears.

"Sorry I wasn't able to look in on her yesterday. I took Walt's boy fishing at his mother's request."

Don't want what you can't have. "Don't trouble yourself about my cat, Mr. Jones. I'm sure you have many other things to occupy your time." How petulant she sounded. She tried to soften her words. "The doctor says she'll mend just fine."

"I'm glad." He removed his suit coat and rolled up the sleeves of his white shirt to his elbows, then leaned back on his forearms, his eyes turning toward the river. "This is prettier country than I'd expected. I like the open spaces, too. Never could abide the big cities."

Curiosity got the better of her. "I haven't been anywhere except Boise City and that was when I was a girl. What was Chicago like?"

"Noisy. Lots of buildings. People everywhere. Crowded streets." He shrugged. "It's not for me." He turned his gaze upon her. "I don't think you'd care for it either, Miss Blessing." He smiled as he added, "Felicity."

She felt the color rush to her cheeks at the sound of her name on his lips.

PRESCOTT LIKED what the blush did to her features. Placing more weight on his left arm, he leaned toward her. "Tell me about your life here. What was Appleton like when you were a girl?"

She was silent a long while before replying, "There wasn't a town when I was born. Just a few farmers, like my grandfather before he died. My grandparents were the first to arrive along this stretch of river, and they were alone for many years, them and my mother. Grandpa Greer planted these apple trees and dug the first irrigation canals himself. My mother sold the orchards when I was small, but Mr. Simpson, the farmer who bought the land, didn't care that I liked to come here to think."

A tender smile played across her mouth, and Prescott realized her lips weren't too full as he'd thought them at first. Instead, her mouth was lush, even a bit provocative when curved upward as it was now.

"Do you have any brothers or sisters?" he asked.

"No, it was just me. There weren't even other children nearby until I was nearly grown."

"What about school?"

"My mother taught me to read and write." Her voice

softened. "Mama taught me everything she could before she died."

He waited a few moments before asking his next question. "Have you ever wanted to leave Appleton?"

She shook her head, then turned her gaze toward the river and western horizon. "Where would I go? This is my home. I don't suppose I'll ever leave."

There was so much she wasn't telling him, and for some reason, he wanted to know it all. He wanted to know why she'd never married. He wanted to know what had put the sadness in her dark, chocolate-colored eyes and what could he do to take it away.

Most of all, Prescott wanted to kiss her. He sat up, testing the thought. He wanted to kiss her? Yes. Yes, he did. It wasn't even surprising. In fact, it seemed quite reasonable. He rose and stepped toward her. She glanced up at him, her eyes wide with uncertainty.

He held out his hand. "Come on. Show me some more of your grandfather's orchards."

She hesitated a moment, then slipped her fingers into his waiting hand and allowed him to pull her to her feet.

He transferred her hand to the crook of his arm, then started walking, following the western-most edge of the orchards. He noticed how easily she kept pace with him, her long legs matching his stride. He also noticed how comfortable it felt to be with her. He was in no hurry to get back to his work as he'd been yesterday with Charlotte. He didn't bother to wonder why. He just knew it was true.

He liked being with Felicity.

FELICITY FELT STRANGELY AT EASE. Oh, her heart still beat faster than normal, but it was a pleasant sort of feeling.

"Tell me, Felicity Blessing. What do you think about Idaho giving women the right to vote?"

It seemed such an odd question. Had she misunderstood him? Of all the things he could have asked her, he wanted to know about women voting? She couldn't help herself. She laughed.

Prescott drew them both to a stop and met her gaze. "You find the right to vote amusing?"

"No." She shook her head as her laughter faded, but her smile remained. "It just seemed so ... so out of the blue. I thought you wanted to know more about the fruit orchards."

"I do, but first answer my other question."

"Well, since you asked, I'll tell you. I think women should have the right to vote in all elections, not just those in Idaho. There are many women like me who must earn wages and support themselves, but we don't have a say in many matters that affect us. Are women less important than other wage earners because of our gender? What the government does affects us as much as it does men. We should have a say in those decisions." She paused. Had she said too much? No, he'd asked for her opinion. "I'm grateful Idaho has seen fit to give women the vote, and I don't intend to ever waste the opportunity."

There was a twinkle in Prescott's eyes. "Admirable sentiments, Miss Blessing. And what do you suppose having the railroad come to Appleton would mean for its citizens?"

She cast a mock frown in his direction. "Mr. Jones, has anyone ever told you your mind works in a peculiar manner?" Then, unable to keep from it, she smiled.

"Miss Blessing—" He placed his hands on her upper arms and drew her toward him. "—has anyone ever told you that you have an irresistible mouth?"

Her breath caught when she realized what was about to happen. Her knees threatened to buckle, but Prescott's grip on her arms steadied her as he drew her closer to him. His mouth upon hers was warm and tender. The kiss lengthened, deepened, sending sparks shooting through her veins.

He had no right to kiss her. She hadn't given him leave to do so. But she didn't want him to stop. His kisses were more wonderful than anything she had ever dreamed.

When at last he lifted his mouth from hers, she opened her eyes to find him watching her with an intense gaze. Then, with the fingers of one hand, he removed her hat pin and Sunday bonnet, dropping them both to the grass at their feet.

This couldn't be happening. Not to her. Not to Felicity Blessing.

Her hair pins followed the hat, and soon, her hair fell free about her shoulders. Prescott threaded his fingers through it, then leaned closer.

"You should always wear your hair down, Felicity," he whispered near her ear, causing gooseflesh to rise on her arm. "It's beautiful." He pulled back and looked her full in the face. "You're beautiful."

PRESCOTT ONLY REALIZED how true the words were as he spoke them. He wondered why he hadn't seen it before now. Tears pooled in her eyes, then slipped onto her cheeks. Tenderly, he kissed them away before claiming her mouth once more with his.

He felt a fierce desire to cherish this woman, to be with her always, and wondered how he could feel so strongly about someone he'd known for such a short time. But wondering how it had happened didn't change what he felt.

It was Felicity who broke the kiss this time. Confusion played across her face as she stared at him. She touched her mouth with her fingertips, her eyes wide with wonder.

"Felicity." He reached for her.

She put out a hand to stop him. "I ... I think it's time for me to go home." She bent down to retrieve her bonnet and hair pins.

"I'll go with you."

She shook her head.

"I should look at Angel."

"Not today, Mr. Jones." She turned and hurried through the trees.

For a long while after she'd gone, Prescott remained at the orchard's edge, remembering how she'd felt in his arms, remembering the sweet taste of her mouth, remembering the luxurious feel of her hair. Most of all, remembering the way he felt.

Prescott Jones had fallen in love.

Chapter 9

*A*ngel Emeline was proud of what she'd accomplished in a short period of time. Not, of course, that she'd had anything to do with the kiss by the river. That had been entirely Prescott's own idea. Still, if she hadn't run out in front of that wagon and been hurt, would that kiss have happened?

If a cat could smile, Angel Emeline would have done so now. Her promotion was almost guaranteed. All that was left was for Prescott to propose marriage to Felicity and for Felicity to accept. And since these two were destined for each other, there was no point in dragging things out. The sooner he proposed, the better.

After all, what could go wrong now?

IN THE DAYS following that memorable Sunday, Prescott came to see Felicity each morning, ostensibly to check on Angel's recovery.

The first morning was awkward. Uncertain about the turbulent emotions roiling inside when Prescott was near, Felicity felt tongue-tied and anxious. She was afraid he might try to kiss her again, and she didn't know whether she wanted him to or not. But he didn't try. He looked at Angel's dressings, said how well she was doing, smiled that devastating smile of his, then left a short while later.

The second morning, it didn't seem quite so strange to have him there. This time, after he looked at Angel, Felicity offered him a cup of coffee before he started to work. Seated opposite each other at the kitchen table, Prescott shared more details about his childhood. About the good years when his parents and siblings had been living. About the difficult years, growing up in the orphanage. About Walt and about Scrapper. About the years after he left Chicago, working and saving so he could one day have a business and a home of his own.

The third morning, Prescott almost forgot to look in on Angel at all. Felicity invited him into the kitchen when he first arrived. This time, it was she who talked about her growing up years. She talked about her mother's unhappiness, about her father's anger and resentment. She found herself revealing things to Prescott Jones that she'd never told another living soul. After he left, she expected to feel regret for speaking so openly, but she didn't.

By the fourth morning, Felicity was waiting for him,

opening the door before he could knock. She wore her
hair down, catching it back with an emerald green ribbon
she'd meant to use on a gown for Mrs. Babcock's shop.
She wore her newest dress. The green one she'd tried on
only once before. This time Prescott saw her in it.

"You look lovely." He placed a feather-light kiss on
her cheek.

Felicity felt lovely when he looked at her that way.

On Friday morning, Felicity met him outside, Angel
in her arms. Before she could say a word, he kissed her on
the mouth. He didn't seem to care that some of the
workmen saw what he did. He smiled and something
wonderful blossomed inside of her.

This was what her mother had told her to wait for,
and now Felicity understood. Why would any woman
settle for less?

"Tell me something," she said as he placed a hand in
the small of her back and guided her along the side of her
house. "What made you decide to come to Appleton after
you'd lived all those other places?"

"I thought it was to be with Walt. He's the closest
thing to family I have." He gazed into her eyes. "But I
think it was to find you, Felicity."

She felt a shiver of joy spread through her. Her
mother had told her never to sell or leave her house
except for love. Maybe it was time to sell it. "Prescott, I've
been thinking—"

"Let me show you how work on the cannery has
progressed this week."

He didn't need to show her, of course. She'd spent

altogether too much time this week looking out the window and watching Prescott as he carried lumber and hammered nails and worked with his crew. She'd memorized the way his black hair gleamed a midnight blue after he cooled himself by dumping water over his head. She knew the color of his work shirts and the precise way his Levi Strauss trousers fit his hips and legs. She could recite by heart the commands he'd called to the men as they worked, could hear the exact timbre of his voice.

Now, as they walked the circumference of the factory, she scarcely looked at the skeleton of the building that would soon rise up around her house. Instead, her gaze returned time and again to Prescott's face. She could see the pride in his eyes, hear the excitement in his words.

"This won't mean success for just me, Felicity. It will be a real boon for all the farmers for miles and miles around. Think of it. They'll be able to sell their goods to folks back on the east coast. The fruit won't spoil in a rail car if an engine breaks down along the way. It can't freeze in the cold or rot in the heat. And the cannery will be big enough to handle whatever is sent to us. Everyone in Appleton will prosper because of it. There'll be more money to buy goods at the mercantile, more money to buy dresses from Mrs. Babcock." He grinned. "Maybe even a dress as pretty as that one you're wearing."

She stopped walking, forcing him to stop, too. "My house is in the way."

"We'll make it work."

"But it would be better if you had my property, as well."

He cupped her chin with his fingers. "Not if you don't want to leave it."

He hadn't told her he loved her. He hadn't offered marriage, but deep in Felicity's heart, she believed that was what he meant. She'd been given her most secret wish — someone to love and someone to love her. Her mother had said not to sell her house for any other reason. She loved Prescott, and he needed this land to succeed. Love had made the decision for her.

"Does your offer still stand, Prescott? Will you buy my house and land?"

He studied her face for a long time before answering, "Yes. If you're sure you want to sell, the J&J Canning Company will buy your place."

Cradling Angel with one arm, Felicity held out her other hand. "I believe a handshake will seal our agreement, Mr. Jones."

———

PRESCOTT THOUGHT a kiss might be a more appropriate way to seal their agreement, but he settled for taking her hand in his. He considered proposing marriage to her that very moment. It was, after all, what he wanted and what he thought she must want, too.

But it was too soon. His plan had always been to start his business, then to take a wife. Just because he'd fallen in love with Felicity Blessing didn't mean he should change those plans. Until the factory was in operation, most of his time and all of his money would be tied up in the business. When he married, he wanted to be able to give plenty of both to his bride. Especially when that bride would be Felicity.

Waiting wasn't going to be easy. With each passing day, his love for her deepened, ripened. Every time he saw her, she grew more lovely in his eyes, more desirable. But wait he must. Releasing her hand, he said, "I'll have Walt draw up the papers this afternoon."

She smiled one of those incredible smiles that transformed her face, and he thought again about kissing her. He planned to do a lot more kissing once they were married.

Chapter 10

*W*alt sat forward in his chair, his face alight with surprise. "You're joking. She's agreed to sell? How did you manage that?"

"I'm hoping it's because she's fallen in love with me." Prescott grinned.

"Because she's— Pres, what have you been up to?"

"As surprising as you might find it, I've been courting Miss Blessing."

Walt frowned.

"Don't worry, my friend. I'm not behaving the scoundrel. I'm quite serious."

"But what about Charlotte? I thought—"

"I'm afraid your sister-in-law and I aren't suited for each other. We don't have anything to talk about when we're alone together. We don't want the same things." He shook his head. "I find Charlotte not very interesting to be with. She's pretty, but it takes more than looks to make a good wife. Marriage wouldn't work for the two of us. We would both be miserable. She knows it as well as I do, although she may not admit it."

"All right. I can accept that. She's not as much like Rebecca as I'd expected. But Miss Blessing? That's the last woman I thought you might fall for."

His grin returned. "What can I say? I'm in love with her. I intend to marry her as soon as the cannery is in operation, if she'll have me."

"Well, I'll be."

Prescott leaned forward in his chair. "I told Felicity you'd draw up the papers for the sale of her house to the J&J Canning Company. She'd like to buy the old Simpson place. I understand their orchards used to belong to her grandfather. I guess she'd like to own them again for sentimental reasons." He didn't mention he'd first kissed Felicity in those same orchards and felt a bit sentimental about them himself. "I looked at the house before coming to see you. It's just the right place to raise a large family."

"I take it you plan to live there, too." Walt chuckled. "Wait 'til I tell Rebecca. She'll never believe this. Not in a million years."

FELICITY STOOD in the middle of her bedroom, gazing at her belongings. It was difficult to comprehend her decision to sell her home. All of her memories were centered around this little place. Soon, probably in a matter of days, it would be leveled. It would disappear and be forgotten.

Was she making a mistake?

Prescott loves you.

How could she be certain of that? He'd kissed her. He'd told her she was lovely. He'd made her feel special. But did he really love her? He'd never mentioned marriage or what was to happen in the days to come. Was there a future for them?

Angel meowed as she sat up on her bed, drawing Felicity's attention. The bandage had been removed from the cat's torso. Long white hair covered any signs of Prescott's careful stitching. Angel even managed to get around by herself now, although she obviously hated the splint that bound her broken leg.

"What is it, pet?" Felicity reached down for the cat. "Am I crazy?"

Of course not. He loves you.

She held the cat at arm's length and stared hard into her green eyes. "Sometimes I'd swear you could talk."

"Reow."

With a shake of her head, she carried Angel into the kitchen and put some scraps from last night's supper into a dish.

"Reow."

She heard the knock on her door and went to answer it, hoping it was Prescott. She knew seeing him would calm her doubts, if only for the time he was with her. But it wasn't Prescott on the other side of her door. It was Charlotte Millard.

"Hello, Miss Blessing." The younger woman smiled. "Do you remember me? I'm Rebecca Johnson's sister."

Felicity's doubts returned three-fold. Looking at Charlotte made her feel dowdy. "Yes. Of course I remember you, Miss Millard."

"I do apologize for calling on you in the middle of the day, but I wanted to speak with you if I may."

"Please. Come in." She opened the door wide and motioned her guest inside.

"What a quaint little house you have." Charlotte breezed past her. "But it is quite small, isn't it? But you are all alone, and I'm sure you won't miss it once it's gone." Charlotte poked her head into the bedroom, then turned around and met Felicity's gaze once more. "You must know how pleased Prescott is that you've decided to sell. He would have done almost anything to get his hands on it. After all, it could mean the success or failure of his cannery. Who knows what he might have said or promised? Such a determined man."

Felicity felt a chill roll up her spine.

"He has completely turned my head with his charms. We have such a delightful time when we're together." She walked toward the door. "Anyway, I don't want to keep you from ... from whatever you were doing. I just wanted to thank you for selling your home. Prescott and I shall be forever grateful. Now, I really must be on my way."

With a ruffle of skirts, she was gone, leaving only a hint of rose-scented cologne in the air as a reminder of her visit.

She was lying.

Had Charlotte lied? It sounded as if she and Prescott had come to an agreement.

Prescott wouldn't use you that way.

But how could she be certain? Why would he even notice her, if not for her home in the center of his property?

You know him, Felicity. Trust your heart. Take a chance on love.

She sat in her straight-backed chair and stared out the window. A moment later, Angel jumped into her lap.

Trust your heart. Take a chance.

She thought back over the time she'd spent with Prescott. She remembered his gentle touch, his warm kisses. She remembered his smile that made her heart thump. She remembered the confidences they'd shared, the times he'd told her she was beautiful. She'd believed him because she loved him.

Maybe she was wrong about him. Maybe she would still be alone when all was said and done. But it was time she took a risk in this life. She was going to believe her heart. She was going to believe in Prescott Jones, no matter what Charlotte Millard said.

Chapter 11

The days had too few hours in them, as far as Prescott was concerned, especially those days immediately following his purchase of Felicity's home. It seemed fate conspired to keep him from having even two minutes alone with her.

On Saturday, the canning equipment arrived by wagon, weeks ahead of schedule, and he had to find a place to store it until the construction on the factory was finished. On Monday, one of his crew fell from a ladder and broke his arm. After the doctor had seen to the injured man, Prescott drove him back to his farm, a half-day's ride away, and didn't return until after nightfall. On Tuesday, a telegram arrived from the railroad, requesting a meeting with proprietors of J&J Canning Company as soon as possible. Prescott and Walt departed for Boise City the next day.

Four days later when the two men returned, Charlotte met them at the door and refused to let

Prescott out of her sight. She was like a prison guard, only prettier and more cloying, flirting and flattering and almost driving him up the wall with her mindless chatter. Finally, unable to escape her any other way, he retired for the night. Tomorrow morning, he would go to see Felicity. He'd missed her.

But when he got up at dawn, he found Charlotte waiting for him in the dining room.

"You're up early, Prescott. I'm glad. I was hoping we could spend the morning together."

"I'm afraid there are pressing matters I must see to."

"But surely you can spend a few hours with me."

"Charlotte, I think we need to—"

"You must know how I feel about you, Prescott."

"No, I'm not sure I do."

"But you must know you've stolen my affections." She blushed, as if embarrassed by her confession. Quite an artful performance. She was a superb actress.

But not superb enough to keep Prescott from guessing how little she cared for him. This was a game to her, a contest she wanted to win. "Charlotte, you're a lovely young woman, but—"

A scowl furrowed her brow. "I won't be toyed with, Prescott."

"I wasn't toying with—"

"You can't intend to throw me over for that old scarecrow."

His jaw clenched. "Be careful what you say."

"She won't have you. I told Miss Blessing you and I have an understanding. I told her you'd do anything to get

her land. And you did, didn't you? You even kissed her to get it. Well, she won't have you now. I made certain of that."

He wanted to shake her until her teeth rattled, and if he didn't leave now, he might do it.

"Achew!" Her face scrunched into a funny expression. "Excuse me. I— Achew!" She sneezed again. And again and again and again.

Prescott glanced toward the open window, and sure enough, there on the window sill sat Angel. He couldn't imagine how she'd managed to get up there with her leg in a splint, but he didn't much care. Grateful for the interruption, he went to the window and scooped the cat into his arms.

"I'd better take you home." He stroked the cat's head. Then he whispered, "Thanks, pal."

Charlotte glared at him when he looked toward her again. Should he mention the red splotches that were appearing on her face and arms? No, she would notice them soon enough.

Subduing a grin, he hurried out of the house.

THE OLD SIMPSON house was enormous. Felicity's few items of furniture seemed to disappear in all the extra space. She moved it around, trying to decide what looked best. She moved it until she realized she was only moving things to fill the empty hours of her day, to keep herself from wondering about Prescott, to keep herself from

believing the worst, to drive Charlotte Millard's suggestions from her mind.

It had been a week since she'd last seen Prescott, and then only for a moment. She'd heard he and Walter Johnson had gone to Boise City, but she hadn't asked why. She wasn't sure she wanted to know.

In the early morning light, Felicity stepped onto the spacious porch of her new home. The air was cool and fresh. Except for the sounds of the river and an occasional trill of a meadowlark, all was silent. She thought this the perfect time of any day.

That was the very moment when Prescott came into view, riding his buckskin, a hat shading his face, Angel cradled in the crook of one arm. Felicity's heart quickened.

He rode up close to the porch before drawing back on the reins. He rested one hand on the pommel, his posture relaxed. Although his eyes were still hidden in the hat brim's shadow, she knew he studied her with an intense gaze. The silence between them seemed to crackle with emotion.

Finally, he said, "You wouldn't believe where I found Angel. You should keep a better eye on her, Miss Blessing. She's only got eight more lives."

She couldn't think of a reply to that.

"You look mighty pretty in the morning light, Felicity."

She ached to be closer to him, but she couldn't seem to move.

He tipped his hat back on his head and peered up at

the sky. "Did I ever tell you what I planned to do when I came to Appleton?" He looked at her again. "I mean besides start the cannery."

She shook her head, not certain whether he had or not, not caring whether he had or not. Just loving the sound of his voice.

"I planned to get the cannery up and running. Then I planned on taking me a wife. I liked the idea of a big house like this one. A big house full of youngsters." He stepped down from the saddle and removed his hat, then set Angel on the first step. With his gaze locked with Felicity's, he moved onto the porch.

She almost stopped breathing.

His voice lowered as he looked into her eyes. "Seems I bought your other place and now I want this one, too. As long as you come part and parcel with it, Miss Blessing. I want to see you standing on this porch every morning with the sunlight in your hair. And I want to see you at night, too, bathed in moonlight."

A tiny gasp—a mixture of surprise and pleasure—escaped her throat.

"What I'm saying is, Felicity, I could have waited to marry some other woman until the factory was in operation, but I can't wait until then to marry you. That's if you'll have me, of course."

He didn't give her a chance to answer before he gathered her into his arms and drew her close, his mouth covering hers. All her uncertainties melted beneath the tender assault. She wrapped her arms around his neck and clung to him while his kisses roamed from her mouth to a sensitive place on her neck. Minutes later — or was it a lifetime? — he broke the kiss to look into her eyes once more. "Will you marry me, Felicity?"

Was it true? Had he spoken those words to her? "Yes, Mr. Jones. I'll marry you."

"Soon?"

"Yes."

"I love you, Miss Blessing."

Miracles did happen, she thought as she was drawn once more into Prescott's embrace. Prayers got answered and wishes came true. If anyone doubted, they need only see what had happened to Felicity, and they would believe.

"I love you, too, Mr. Jones. I always will."

Epilogue

*A*ngel Emeline waited nervously while the Archangel in Charge of Prayer Assistance reviewed the file before him. Occasionally, Archie murmured a thoughtful, "Hmm," which never failed to send a shiver of apprehension down Angel Emeline's spine.

She'd wanted this promotion so badly. She'd been counting on being an Angel, Second Grade. Had she failed despite her best efforts?

"Well, Emeline."

She swallowed hard as her superior closed the file and lifted his gaze to meet hers.

"I see Felicity and Prescott have found one another."

"Yes, sir."

"Their wedding appears to have been quite a celebration for the citizens of Appleton, coming on the same day as the announcement that the railroad was coming up their way."

"Yes, sir. It certainly was. A great day."

"Are you aware their first child will be born in the spring?"

"No, sir. I hadn't heard. That's wonderful."

"Yes, it is. Wonderful, indeed. I foresee a great future for the Jones family. I am pleased with the way things turned out."

Angel Emeline's nerves began to calm. Archie was pleased with what she'd done.

Her superior flipped open the file and glanced at the papers inside a second time. "However, Emeline, some of your methods were a bit ... unorthodox. Wouldn't you say?"

So much for calming her nerves. "Yes, sir."

"That poor cat could have been killed when she ran in front of those horses pulling that wagon."

"I tried to be careful, sir, but I'm afraid I wasn't used to having four legs. My timing was off and I—"

"Yes. Yes. I know." He smiled.

Angel Emeline couldn't believe it. Archie smiled? In the ages she'd known him, she couldn't recall ever seeing Archie smile.

"The important thing is you helped Felicity discover the answer to her prayer. And Prescott found the right woman in the process. That's very gratifying to me. I hoped he would find happiness. He was always a brave lad and he had a soft spot in his heart for strays."

Angel Emeline leaned forward, a suspicion sparking to life. Was it possible? No. It couldn't be. Archie?

He read her thoughts. "Yes, I was Scrapper. That was

my last earthly assignment. I became rather fond of the boy during those years. I knew he would grow into a fine man."

"But I didn't think you ever left these chambers."

"Even an Archangel in Charge must be concerned with helping those on Earth. Besides, it gives me perspective when I'm assessing the performance of others." He folded his hands in front of him. "I shall be processing your promotion papers immediately."

Angel Emeline grinned. She'd succeeded. Angel, Second Grade. She'd done it. She'd made two people happy, and she'd earned her promotion. There couldn't be a nicer ending than that.

"May I tell the others, sir?"

He nodded. "Yes, you may tell them."

She rose from her chair.

"But before you go, Emeline, about Miss Millard's rash..."

Note to Reader

This novella was written for a bit of fun. It is pure fantasy and not meant to be anything more than that. The story definitely isn't theologically correct when it comes to angels.

The angels of the Bible are portrayed as quite different from Angel Emeline. Whenever angels appeared to mankind in the Bible, they did it in a human form, and the Bible is what we should trust for an understanding of all things spiritual, including angels.

Still, I hope you enjoyed reading this romantic bit of whimsy. It's a story that made me smile as I wrote it.

Robin Lee Hatcher

You might also like . . .

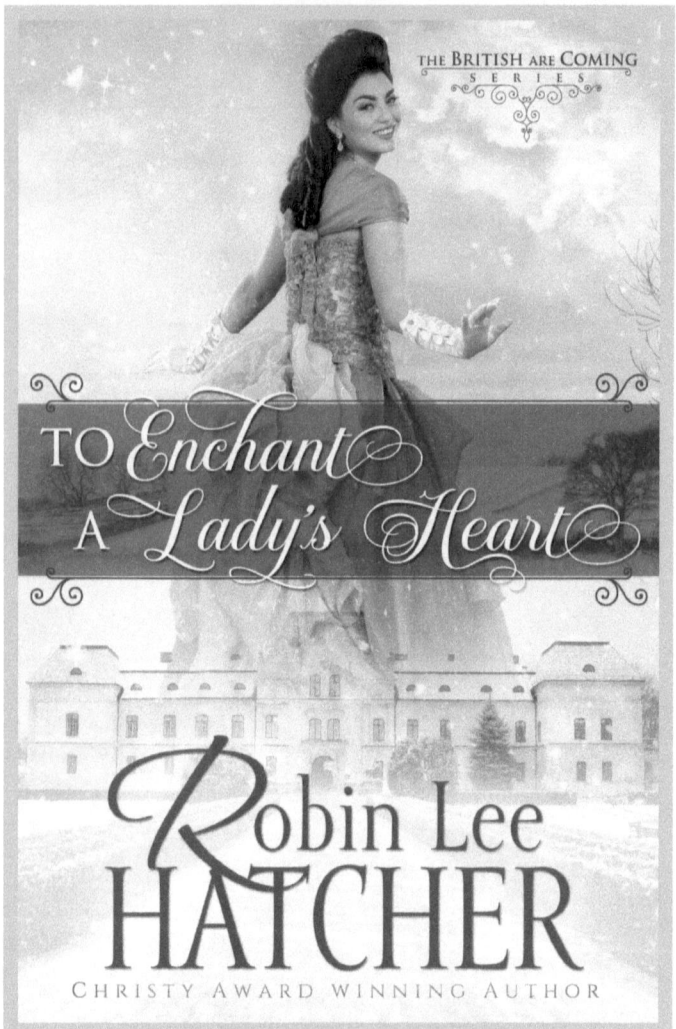

To Enchant a Lady's Heart
BOOK ONE, THE BRITISH ARE COMING

Prologue

London, Fall 1894

The Blakeslee ballroom glittered as couples swirled around the dance floor. Laughter and voices rose above the music, creating a loud din.

Standing alone, not far from the refreshments, Eliza Southwick observed the festive gathering and wished herself back home at Briar Park. Her new ballgown was too tight across the shoulders, and her dancing slippers pinched her toes. No longer a young debutante, she wasn't eagerly sought after by the eligible men in attendance. That might have stung if she'd met a gentleman she found interesting. She hadn't. Not at this ball nor any other she'd attended since her introduction to society.

She covered her mouth with a gloved hand, hiding a yawn of boredom behind it.

The official London Season had ended over two months ago, but people always returned to the city for Lord and Lady Blakeslee's Autumn Ball. Even Eliza's father wouldn't have missed it, especially not while he had hopes that his daughter would capture the attention of a titled lord.

Looking away from the dance floor, she caught sight of her father, deep in conversation with the Earl of Hooke, Lord Whitcombe. The earl had an unmarried son. She'd met Sebastian Whitcombe on more than one occasion, and she liked him well enough. But she didn't think they would suit each other. For one thing, Sebastian didn't seem to share her passion for horses nor did he seem to like reading, another of her interests. Did her father know that about him? Did he know it about her? Did he care?

She closed her eyes as she stepped closer to a large parlor palm. Behind her, rain still splattered against the windows, but she couldn't hear it falling now. She wished she could, for it was a sound that soothed her when she felt uncertain...and unloved.

A memory flitted through her mind. The memory of an evening in the stables at Briar Park several months ago and of the man who had waited and watched with her while a foal was born.

Dear God, please send the right man into my life. Please send me someone to love.

Chapter One

Hooke Manor, Winter 1895

The earl wishes to see you in the library, Mr. Faulkner. At once."

Without comment, Adam gave the black mare a pat on the shoulder, then left the stall, following the young footman out of the stables and toward one of the rear entrances to the manor house. He leaned into the bitter wind that sliced through his coat, all the while wishing he'd gone to London with Sebastian that morning. Anything would be better than what awaited him in the library. The Earl of Hooke had been in a foul temper for days, and there was only one reason he'd sent for Adam now. He wanted help, the sort of help Adam didn't want to give.

Once inside the manor, he went straight to the library. He didn't remove his coat or take time to wash up. The earl was not a patient man in the best of circumstances.

"You sent for me, my lord." Adam stopped inside the doorway.

An imposing man in his late sixties with steel gray hair and eyes, the earl paced back and forth in front of a stone fireplace. Finally he stopped and glared in Adam's direction. "You knew Sebastian went to London?"

"Yes, my lord. He told me before he left." Adam paused before adding, "He asked me to go with him. He wanted to open his house."

"Blast that boy."

Sebastian Whitcombe, Viscount Willowthorpe, was not a boy. Adam's half-brother was in his early thirties.

"Why didn't you stop him?" the earl demanded. "You know we have guests arriving tomorrow."

"Yes, my lord. I know. But he was determined."

"Blast." The older man spun toward the blazing fire. "It's time he settled down and married. It's time he had children of his own. He has a duty to this family, to Hooke Manor."

Adam said nothing. When the earl was like this, no words were required. In truth, prudence demanded silence.

The earl gripped the mantel with both hands and leaned closer to the fire, his entire body rigid. After a long, silent spell, he drew a deep breath and faced Adam again. "I'll see that he returns home at once."

"Do you want me to go to London?"

"No." The earl shook his head. "No, I want you to stay here. We have guests arriving. *I* will go to London. I have things to say to my son that must be said in person. You will stay here and assist Amanda with our guests."

"You want me to assist?"

"Yes. Sebastian and I will return on Wednesday, well before the rest of our guests arrive. But Lord George and his daughter will be here tomorrow. I don't want Amanda to face them alone."

Uncomfortable as he was at the thought, Adam answered, "As you wish, my lord."

The earl sighed. "Why couldn't that boy be more like

you?" He turned to the fireplace, and by his demeanor, Adam knew he'd been dismissed.

The earl was wrong, of course. Sebastian and Adam were more similar than their father acknowledged. They looked enough alike to be full brothers, and once, over a decade earlier, they'd been mistaken for twins, despite the three years that separated them. In addition to their similar looks, they had matching senses of humor and enjoyed riding fast horses.

There was, however, a not-so-small difference between the half-brothers. Sebastian was a gentleman and the heir to the earldom while Adam had been born on the wrong side of the blanket.

Another difference was Sebastian's reluctance to marry. Especially to marry someone deemed suitable by their father. Unfortunately, the young woman their father had chosen for Sebastian had captured a piece of Adam's heart months ago, a fact he had revealed to no one.

Why would he reveal it? He couldn't act upon his feelings, no matter how much he would like to. He was, after all, the illegitimate son of the Earl of Hooke. He'd been treated kindly since coming to live at the manor at the age of four. In many ways he'd been treated as an equal to Sebastian. He'd received an education. He'd become the stable manager while still in his twenties, and his income was generous. In the right setting, he was accepted by Sebastian's closest friends with nary a disapproving glance.

And yet Adam knew his place.

There was also the matter of Eliza's dowry, not to mention the stallion she would bring to Hooke Manor. The earl wanted the dowry, of course, but he coveted the horse. And to get them both Sebastian must marry Miss Southwick.

As Adam returned to the stables, he reminded himself that his half-brother was a good man. Sebastian might not want to marry Eliza at present, but he would grow to care for her, given a little time. How could he help it once he stopped objecting simply because their father liked her?

There was so much to like about Eliza Southwick, too. She was pretty in an unconventional way. Petite and curvaceous, she had a heart-shaped face, dark hair, and a musical laugh. But it was the sparkle of mischief in her eyes that had drawn Adam's attention the previous year. That and a passion for horses that matched his own.

In fact, it was horses that had caused them to meet. Eliza had slipped away from the guests at the Briar Park house party to visit the stables where a favorite mare was about to foal. Adam had been in the stables as well, attending to the Whitcombe horses. Moonlight had ushered Eliza through the open stable door, silvering the gown she'd worn. She'd looked like an angel, and Adam had never recovered.

He gave his head a quick shake, driving away the memory. He couldn't continue to think about Eliza that way. Not if she was to be Sebastian's bride. And that would surely happen. The earl didn't give up on a plan once his mind was set.

Countess—the mare he'd been attending earlier and one of the finest horses on his father's estate—greeted Adam with a huff of air and the stomp of a hoof. He ran a hand along the mare's back but found it difficult to focus his thoughts on the animal. They kept wandering to Sebastian...and to Miss Eliza Southwick. Frustrated, he turned and gave instructions to the stable boy who waited nearby. Then Adam left the horse barn, this time going to his small cottage, wishing he could drown his thoughts in a bottle of spirits but knowing instead that he would spend a long evening staring into the fire, filled with regret.

Weak morning sunlight spilled through the windows of the bedchamber as Eliza stared at the looking glass. But she took no note of her reflection therein. Her thoughts were instead upon her father and the days ahead of her.

At twenty-four, Eliza was beyond the age when her father, the third son of the Marquis of Heathborough, had expected her to make an appropriate match. Society agreed. Too many London Seasons had passed for her to be taken seriously by most gentlemen in search of a wife. They viewed her as unwanted goods, despite the wealth of her father, Lord George Southwick. No man had proposed to her in her first season or those that followed. Her own fault for keeping them at bay. So why should any man choose her now? There were too many younger, more beautiful girls to choose from with each new year.

Eliza wondered what her father had offered the Earl of Hooke to make her desirable enough for a match with Viscount Willowthorpe. The price must be exceedingly high.

Tears pooled in her eyes. She would like nothing more than to marry, but she so wished it could be for love. If not love, respect. Or at the very least that a man might want her for herself and not to improve his purse or his riding stables.

"Miss?"

She blinked away the unshed tears before turning toward the door.

Her maid stepped into the room. "Your father says for you to come at once. Are you ready?"

"I am, Mary. Thank you." She retrieved her gloves from a nearby table and tugged them onto her hands. Then she pointed to a bag. "That is the last one."

"I'll see to it."

Head held high, Eliza made her way along the hallway and down the stairs to the main entrance where her father waited, impatience in his eyes. He gave her a quick, appraising look. Apparently she passed the inspection for he gave a curt nod and turned to lead the way outside.

Patches of snow from a rare late winter storm lingered beneath trees and in the shadows of buildings, and a cold wind assaulted Eliza as she followed her father to the carriage. The gusts cut through her cloak like a knife. She would be thankful for the blankets and furs inside the coach, but despite them, she knew she would be chilled to the bone before they reached Hooke Manor in the afternoon. She shuddered to think what it would be like for their servants who had to make the journey in the elements. At least her maid and her father's valet would be inside the second coach that carried all of their luggage. Luggage packed with enough clothing to last them for a variety of occasions for more than a week. Assuming everything went as her father planned, Eliza would need each and every ensemble.

George Southwick was not one to engage in idle conversation if it could be avoided, so Eliza was left to her own thoughts as they set off across the countryside. Those thoughts, despite her best efforts to thwart them, settled immediately on Sebastian Whitcombe. Without question, the viscount was handsome, and the times she'd been in his company, she'd found him charming and engaging. All of the other unmarried females in England felt the same about him, no doubt.

So why would he want to marry Eliza?

Again, she wondered what her father had offered for his only daughter, above and beyond the expected dowry. And that made her feel like a horse at auction. A rather pathetic view of herself, she supposed, especially since the arrangement was not unusual. It was the way things had been done among the aristocracy for centuries. Marriages were more often about position and money rather than affection. Marrying for love had never been the expected practice for those of rank. Perhaps not for commoners either.

If only Mother were alive to help me sort this out.

She closed her eyes, picturing her mother. Gwendolyn Southwick had been more than a great beauty. Exuding elegance and grace, she had also possessed a gentle and kind spirit, beloved by all who knew her but especially by her daughter. Eliza had been only ten when her mother died while giving birth to William, the surviving son and heir to the Southwick estate. It seemed to Eliza that she'd ceased to exist at that same moment her mother passed away.

Looking across the carriage at her father, she felt the sadness in her chest increase. He wasn't cruel to her. Only indifferent. And that cut deeper than cruelty. She was, after all, a daughter and not a son. Her role was to marry well. It mattered little whether she was happy.

To Enchant a Lady's Heart
Book One
The British Are Coming series

"Hatcher's newest novella offers the same sweet romance and page-turning storyline you've come to expect from this author if you've read her before. If you haven't, you're in for a treat! *To Enchant a Lady's Heart* is, in a word, well...*enchanting*."

— Deborah Raney, author of *Breath of Heaven* and *A Nest of Sparrows*

"Robin Lee Hatcher opens her new series, The British Are Coming, with a delightful novella that's sure to capture readers' hearts. The characters are unique, and the plot is engaging from start to finish. This promises to be a fun series with a clash of cultures as the British characters travel to the Western United States. Readers who are looking for well written historical romance will enjoy this novella and the novels to follow."

— Carrie Turansky, award-winning author of *No Journey Too Far* and *The Legacy of Longdale Manor*

About the Author

Robin Lee Hatcher is the best-selling author of over 85 books. Her well-drawn characters and heartwarming stories of faith, courage, and love have earned her both critical acclaim and the devotion of readers. Her numerous awards include the Christy Award for Excellence in Christian Fiction, the RITA® Award for Best Inspirational Romance, Romantic Times Career Achievement Awards for Americana Romance and for Inspirational Fiction, the Carol Award, the 2011 Idahope Writer of the Year, and Lifetime Achievement Awards from both Romance Writers of America® (2001) and American Christian Fiction Writers (2014). *Catching Katie* was named one of the Best Books of 2004 by the Library Journal.

When not writing, Robin enjoys being with her family, spending time in the beautiful Idaho outdoors, Bible art journaling, reading books that make her cry, watching romantic movies, knitting, and decorative planning. A mother and grandmother, Robin makes her home on the outskirts of Boise, sharing it with a demanding Papillon dog and a persnickety tuxedo cat.

Learn more about Robin and her books by visiting her website at robinleehatcher.com

You can also find out more by joining her on social media.

Also by Robin Lee Hatcher

Stand Alone Titles

Books set in Kings Meadow

A Promise Kept

Love Without End

Whenever You Come Around

I Hope You Dance

Keeper of the Stars

Books set in Thunder Creek

You'll Think of Me

You're Gonna Love Me

The Sisters of Bethlehem Springs Series

A Vote of Confidence

Fit to Be Tied

A Matter of Character

Legacy of Faith series

Who I am With You

Cross My Heart

How Sweet It Is

For a full list of books, visit robinleehatcher.com